TOKYO GIRL

BRIAN HARVEY

A Frank Ryan Mystery

RAVEN BOOKS
an imprint of
ORCA BOOK PUBLISHERS

Library and Archives Canada Cataloguing in Publication

Harvey, Brian J., 1948–, author
Tokyo girl / Brian Harvey.
(Rapid reads)

Issued also in print and electronic formats.
ISBN 978-1-4598-1076-1 (pbk.).—ISBN 978-1-4598-1077-8 (pdf).—
ISBN 978-1-4598-1078-5 (epub)

I. Title. II. Series: Rapid reads
PS8615.A77383T65 2016   C813'.6   C2016-900447-3
C2016-900448-1

First published in the United States, 2016
Library of Congress Control Number: 2016931820

Summary: In this murder mystery unlikely sleuth Frank Ryan
navigates the unfamiliar culture and structure of Tokyo. (RL 5.6)

*Orca Book Publishers is dedicated to preserving the environment and has
printed this book on Forest Stewardship Council® certified paper.*

Orca Book Publishers gratefully acknowledges the support for
its publishing programs provided by the following agencies:
the Government of Canada through the Canada Book Fund and the
Canada Council for the Arts, and the Province of British Columbia
through the BC Arts Council and the Book Publishing Tax Credit.

Cover design by Jenn Playford
Cover photography by iStock.com

ORCA BOOK PUBLISHERS
www.orcabook.com

Printed and bound in Canada.

19 18 17 16 • 4 3 2 1

"The nail that stands up must be pounded down." —*Japanese proverb*

Looking for the Moon

"That's *so* much better," I said, trying to make it sound like I meant it. At the keyboard, Mrs. Ogawa made a quick ducking motion, as though someone had zinged a baseball at her head. I'm pretty sure this meant "I know you're lying. But thanks anyway." She folded her small hands in her lap and awaited instructions. She was wearing her "home" uniform: gray jumper, furry, pink slippers and a powder-blue apron that said *Loving Food Enjoy*.

Ducking my own head was something I did every Wednesday, when I came to Mrs. Ogawa's apartment. I didn't really need to.

The door frame was big enough for most Westerners, and I'm only five eleven. But I ducked anyway, even after I'd reduced my height by taking off my shoes. Maybe because the space I was entering was so ridiculously small. Maybe because I was afraid of doing some kind of humiliating damage. Or maybe it was just Japan. The whole country made me feel like ducking.

Mrs. Ogawa's husband was a wholesaler of fish cakes in the famous Tsukiji seafood market. Or something like that. I'd never met him. Even if I had, I probably wouldn't have asked about his place of business. If I'd known that my last night in Japan would be spent in his fish market, I would have.

His wife had her heart set on learning *Clair de Lune*, by Claude Debussy. We'd been at it together for two months and were closing in on page two. I didn't have the heart to tell her what was coming on page three. Mrs. Ogawa had applied herself equally hard to learning English, so we could communicate after a fashion. But these piano lessons were a challenge for both of us.

"Try thinking of a full moon," I said. Mrs. Ogawa ducked another baseball. "You're standing on the shore of a lake, the moon's risen, and it's just pouring this warm light over the water." She ducked again. "As though..." I stopped. What was I thinking? There were probably another fifty Mrs. Ogawas in this building alone. Ditto for the building next door, ditto as far as I could see into the smog outside. A whole army of Ogawa-sans. All of them seemed determined to learn *Clair de Lune*, or Beethoven's *Moonlight Sonata*. But here was the problem: the moon in Tokyo, if you saw it at all, was about as brilliant as a dirty twenty-five-watt bulb. Neon light and air pollution took care of the moon. As for a deserted lake—forget it.

We sat in silence while I struggled for words. Together we listened to the muffled roar of the Chuo Expressway half a mile from the Ogawa family's tenth-floor apartment in Setagaya. Mrs. Ogawa's apartment was tagged in my smartphone—otherwise I'd never be able to find it.

Mrs. Ogawa paid me well. So did the other Mrs. Ogawas who'd seen my ad and convinced their husbands to allow a *gaijin*—a foreigner—into the family home for a weekly shot of culture. I wanted her to get her money's worth. But it was in moments like this that I felt the most alien in Japan. Real communication seemed remote.

"We need a little more emotion," I finally said. "You know what I mean? Emotion?" Mrs. Ogawa looked at her hands, and her head bobbed, ever so slightly. Everyone knew what emotions were, even if they dealt with them differently. "May I?"

I tapped her on the shoulder, and she shot to attention. I slid onto the piano bench.

"Lake. Moon. All alone." She stood behind me and I played the first few bars. *Clair de Lune* really is a beautiful piece, even if it was written for a pianist with hands twice the size of my student's. I could hear Mrs. Ogawa breathing behind me. Or maybe it was the Chuo Expressway. I decided to let Debussy do the talking. I didn't stop until I'd played the whole piece through.

Then I just sat there. Mrs. Ogawa's breathing sounded different. I turned around. She had one hand over her nose and mouth. There were tear tracks down both checks. She sniffed. The lesson was over.

"Thank you, Frank-san," she said from behind her hand. She darted into her miniature kitchen and extracted five thousand yen from a drawer the way she always did. Then she presented the banknotes to me formally, with both hands and a little bow.

Japan was still a cash-dominated society. Every housewife seemed to have her own private stash somewhere. One of my students kept it underneath the rice cooker.

Mrs. Ogawa's money was wet with her tears. That was as close as I was going to get to knowing what she was really thinking. She darted to the door, smiled bravely while I crammed my big feet into my shoes, then lowered her head while I lumbered out.

When I reached street level, the roar of the city engulfed me and the midday heat had me sweating in seconds. Middle-aged ladies hid from the sun beneath umbrellas and pizza-sized plastic visors. Elegant grandmothers pulled wheeled shopping bags. It was early June. The national tie loosening and boozing of cherry blossom festival was over. But the city still had another ten degrees of cloying heat in store for us.

Spotless cars crawled beneath a yellowish haze. Most of them were white. One of Tokyo's millions of silent silver bicycles blew past me on the sidewalk, its basket jammed with shopping bags. I staggered into a concrete telephone pole.

I had two free hours before my next student. I'd need all of that time to get to Ota district by train, grab a cheap bowl of ramen to fortify me, and cover the last few blocks on foot. And, to be honest, I needed that time to get ready for Akiko.

When I said that all my students were exactly like Mrs. Ogawa, I left out Akiko, who was in a category of her own. Akiko lived in a house, not an apartment. And she'd spent enough time outside Japan to learn excellent idiomatic English. Akiko wore designer jeans and probably didn't even own an apron. She took her lessons on a gleaming Yamaha grand that had a room of its own. Akiko had looks, brains and more than a little talent. So far, I'd never seen any sign that she had a job. But somebody must have paid for the cosmetic surgery that had given her that narrow nose and those Western-looking eyes.

Akiko was complicated. Every time I entered her house, I felt like ducking, all right—ducking out. And every time I said goodbye and walked back to the train station, I found myself wondering why I was still in Japan at all.

Akiko

Being a tourist in Japan is easy. In my case, I chose Japan because I needed to disappear somewhere safe. It was a no-brainer.

After what happened to me in Nanaimo, I started seeing villains everywhere. My gig as a late-night jazz pianist was over. I started giving the harbor a wide berth, in case someone might snatch me again. Just opening my own apartment door involved double-checking the latch, a lot of deep breaths and one hand on the bear spray I kept in my pocket. It was too bad. I liked Nanaimo. The city fit me like an old pair of jeans. But I'd tripped over those frayed cuffs, and I needed out.

According to the Internet, my chances of being assaulted or kidnapped were lowest in the Nordic countries, in New Zealand and in Japan. It was snowing in Nanaimo the day I did my research, and Denmark and Sweden would just be more of the same. No thanks. All the pictures of New Zealand looked just like British Columbia, and I wanted change. That left Japan, where even if you got incredibly unlucky and someone bopped you over the head, they'd probably say "Excuse me" first.

But what if I ran into Kaz Nakamura? Even if he had gone back to Japan, statistics took care of that one. Japan has 127 million people. The mathematical odds of meeting Kaz were a bullet train of zeroes with a lonely numeral one at the end. Kaz and I had parted ways on a snowy night in Vancouver, and I would never see him again.

I gave my Nanaimo landlord six months' rent and bought a ticket for Tokyo.

I arrived at the end of March. It was just two weeks after an earthquake under the Pacific Ocean had driven a thirty-foot wall of water—a tsunami—through the coastal city of Fukushima. The tidal wave hurdled a seawall. It tossed freighters and ferries ashore like bathtub toys and left buses on hospital roofs. And it turned a nuclear power plant into a leaking, radioactive time bomb. Japan had obviously used up its statistical share of bad luck. I would be fine.

And I was. You couldn't blame the country for being twitchy about after-shocks and radiation. Maybe that's why nobody paid much attention to me. Every week I moved to a cheaper hotel, adjusting to my new surroundings and putting off my return.

It's hard to imagine how thirteen million people keep their cool, but the Japanese in Tokyo manage it. Nobody makes eye contact. The train platforms can be packed, but nobody speaks. Merchants smile and bow. All of this, I began to realize, suited me fine. When an Australian I met in the Excelsior Caffé offered to sublet me his bachelor apartment, I took it. It was that simple.

That was two months ago. Today I was sitting in a noodle shop three minutes from Akiko's house, fueling up. You can't go wrong with a bowl of ramen. This place was typical. Six stools faced a scarred wooden counter and a grim-looking chef in a headband and a cloud of steam. He was flinging noodles and vegetables and slices of pork into bowls of his secret broth.

I ordered a Kirin. The place was full of men inhaling wet noodles. I never could do the slurping thing—usually I ended up speckling my shirt with broth. The customers kept their eyes on the TV high up in one corner. A man in a tight suit was saying something alarming about radiation.

I knew it was alarming because Japanese TV news features lots of graphics and endlessly repeated footage of scenes of disaster. You didn't need to understand Japanese to figure out that Tokyo was having another scare about radioactive tap water. On the screen, bottled water flew off the shelves, and housewives dithered over contaminated vegetables. I finished my beer and left a thousand-yen note on the counter. The stylish residential area where Akiko lived was just around the corner.

Ota district was a lot different from Mrs. Ogawa's neighborhood. The streets were narrow and painted with bewildering markings: arrows, dashes, dots, diamonds, numbers. It was like walking through a game of snakes and ladders. Every house was gated. The lots were small, and few of the houses had windows facing the street.

This was Japan, where people looked inward.

From the street, Akiko's house was a slanted field of shiny blue roof tiles above an iron gate set into a stone wall. The silver Lexus in the tiled carport looked as though it had never left the showroom. I pushed the unmarked button set into the wall, and the gate swung silently open. A path of crushed stone led through a manicured garden with miniature cypress trees that trailed above a mossy pool. A Tokyo crow, big as a raven, muttered at me from the roof.

I squatted and watched two koi chase each other's tails beneath a sprinkling of cherry petals. One fish was red splashed dramatically on white, like blood. The other was a solid-gold submarine.

"Do you like fish, Frank?"

Akiko's bare brown toes were right next to me. I struggled to my feet. She knelt and paddled a long finger in the water, and the golden fish turned majestically to nuzzle it. "This one is my favorite. I call him Sunshine."

Akiko was willowy where Mrs. Ogawa was stout. She'd pulled her long hair into a ponytail that shot skyward before falling down her back. The top half of her was draped in an upscale poncho of earth-colored linen. The rest of her was inside strategically frayed jeans. It was hot in her tiny tropical garden, and I was sweating like a sailor.

"I wouldn't know what to do with a pet fish," I said. Akiko stood and smiled. That smile was the only part of her I felt comfortable with. It was lopsided. Maybe the surgeon had slipped. Somebody else had slipped too, and recently, because one of Akiko's remanufactured eyes was the color of a ripe fig. It was also swollen shut. She caught me looking, but her smile never wavered.

I walked into a door," she said. I followed her ponytail across the polished flagstones.

Each step left a fleeting footprint on the hot stone, as though she'd been waiting for me in the refrigerator.

Akiko's piano was better than anything I could ever have owned, a full nine gleaming feet that sat on a purple Persian rug. The only natural light came from a narrow, ceiling-level window that ran the length of one earth-tone wall. A single spotlight lit the keyboard. The only other piece of furniture was a cowhide-and-chrome chair that probably cost a month of my earnings back home. The walls were bare. It was a Zen garden for music.

I sank into the cool leather and watched her bare feet go up and down on the Yamaha's pedals. Someone needed to tell Akiko to wear shoes to play piano, but it wasn't going to be me. She was playing Chopin, one of his weepier preludes, a piece we'd been working on for a month.

I wondered what it was like to read music with one eye.

The notes were all there, but I knew without even looking at Akiko that something was missing. Akiko had talent, but today she had tension too. Not a good combination for a musician.

I got up. My pants stuck to my legs. I took one slender, locked wrist in my fingers. "Don't stop playing," I said. "Try to let go."

But she did stop. And it wasn't because I was bent over her wrist like a kindly doctor. It was because there was someone else in the room.

A reading journal

A quiz what I have read and vrahulary

A 7-senten

An Offer You Can't Refuse

The guy was big for a Japanese man, taller even than me. Like most Japanese men, he still had plenty of hair, swept high off his forehead and shot with silver. And he definitely had his own sense of style. He wore a cream-colored silk suit over a collarless pink shirt, a black bolo tie and retro Ray-Bans on a gold chain. I could see pale flesh through black silk socks.

I had time to take in the details, because he didn't say a word. He just stared at the *gaijin* with soup spots on his shirt and his hand on Akiko's wrist. Then he took the sunglasses off. Nobody had done any surgery on this guy's eyes. They were like slits. I wondered how he could see at all. But it was his protruding lower lip that worried me most. If the three of us were fish, Akiko and I would be sardines. He would be a barracuda.

"This is my father." Akiko stood up. She said something in Japanese. I heard *piano* and *teacher* and my name. The emotion that Akiko was having trouble channeling into music seemed to be coming out fine now. The man made a deep grunting noise, put down the crocodile-skin briefcase he was carrying and stuck out a hand.

Jeweled rings dug into my palm. I wondered which one of them had caught Akiko on the eyeball. He didn't have a ring on his little finger because his little finger was missing.

"*Hajimemashite*," I said, which I was pretty sure meant "nice to meet you."

Then he and Akiko had a little chat. I looked around. The walls were framed into panels using a warm blond wood that I figured for cypress. The surfaces were covered in some kind of subtly pebbled paper in a washed-out moss green. The room went with Akiko, not with the guy barking at her. The only family resemblance I could see was in how vigorously they argued. Finally Akiko turned to me.

"He says, if you're my teacher, play something." She half smiled. "I suggest something calm."

I sat down and played the Chopin piece we'd been working on. It wasn't long, but it felt like forever with Barracuda-san behind my back. Akiko settled into the leather chair as though this kind of thing happened every day. I finished the prelude and waited for knuckles to connect with my ear.

"Unh." It was a deep, punched-in-the-gut kind of sound, one of the bewildering variations on groans and grunts that Japanese people make. I had no idea what it meant. He followed up with a volley of Japanese.

"He doesn't like classical music," Akiko said. "He prefers jazz."

"Me too."

Akiko looked at me. "You never told me that, Frank."

"You never asked."

She said something to the man. He made that sucker-punched grunt again, then approached the piano. In English, he said slowly, "You know 'My Funny Valentine'?"

Here was one argument for his being her father—they both seemed to go for the tearjerker tunes. "You got it," I said. I let both of them have it, the first jazz I'd played since arriving in Japan. And it came in a torrent. I gave the tune its full measure of gift-wrapped misery. It was like being back in Kaz's little bar in Nanaimo again, the whiskey taking the edges off a long day and Kaz's sax dipping and swooping beside me.

When I'd finished, the man cleared his throat and set off on another long back-and-forth with Akiko. He sounded slightly less murderous now.

"He has a job for you," Akiko said.

"I already have a job. I was trying to do it when your—this person showed up."

"I won't translate that," Akiko said.

"What kind of job?"

"One of the bars he owns. In Kichijoji."

"I live in Kichijoji."

"That's why he found you a place there. He has a vacancy for a late-night jazz pianist."

"How many bars does he own?"

"No idea."

"But the one in my neighborhood just happens to need a new piano player? Come on."

"Take it," Akiko said.

He did look like the sort of person who could make things happen quickly. And I wanted to do it. Playing a single sappy tune on a good piano had been like a jolt of twelve-year-old whiskey after a long dry spell.

"I'll think about it," I said. Akiko looked at me the way the way you'd look at a not-too-bright six-year-old.

"I'll tell him you're very grateful, and ask when you can start."

I still had to know one thing. "What happened to the other piano player?"

Akiko laughed and said something to the man. He grunted. They conferred. She turned back to me.

"A problem with one of his fingers." Then the Ray-Bans were back on and the crocodile briefcase back in his hand. I decided to change the subject.

"It's beautiful." I pointed to the brief-case. Barracuda-san grinned.

"You like? I kill him. In Brazil." He ran his hand over the pebbled surface, and Akiko rolled her reconstructed eyes.

"On safari with his friends," she said. "Watch out he doesn't skin you too." Then he was gone. There was a lingering smell of expensive cologne. I slumped into the leather chair.

"Father, my ass," I said under my breath. But Akiko had good ears.

"I know what that means," she said. "I did a whole year of English idioms when I was abroad. Now I'll give you one."

"And that is?"

"Never look a gift horse in the mouth."

I was impressed. I told her so. "You've seen *The Godfather*, I'm guessing."

"More than once."

"Then you know the scene where the don says, *I'm gonna make you an offer you can't refuse*. Another interesting idiom, don't you think?"

Akiko touched the bruise around her eye. "Tell me about it," she said. She went to another room and returned with payment for her lesson. Cash, like Mrs. Ogawa, like all my students. But I suspected Akiko's private bank was bigger than all of the others put together.

Tom and Mary

And that was how I began my brief career as house pianist in the Tom and Mary Jazz Lounge, near Inokashira Park in Kichijoji.

Inokashira Park is a big part of living in Kichijoji. The place has pedal boats and performers. Artists display everything from hand-painted umbrellas to crickets folded from straw. The cherry trees blaze in spring, and the maples along the river flame out spectacularly in fall. To get to the park, you walk down a bustling pedestrian mall. A warren of side streets lead to underground restaurants and bars and places like the Tom and Mary.

The buildings are so close together you'd have to turn sideways to walk between them. They look like they would go down like dominoes in a decent earthquake. The street is strung in a spider's web of electrical lines and lit by fixtures that look like old-fashioned gas lamps. Kichijoji is upscale. *fancy*

I'd always assumed the Tom and Mary was a slightly shady hotel, but if you pushed *down* instead of *up* in the tiny elevator, you skipped the sketchy rooms and ended up in a jazz lounge instead. I sometimes wondered whether spending so much time underground was very smart or very stupid. But the place was always full. Maybe that meant it was super safe. Or maybe some Japanese people wanted to be listening to jazz when the roof fell in.

As for Akiko's "father," his name was Mr. Goto. He was working out surprisingly well. My first night on the job, he was all business, if you could ignore his outfit.

The cream linen suit had been replaced by a shiny black one with wide lapels from the seventies and a brown leather vest peeking out from underneath the jacket. He even kept his shoes on, a pair of shiny black wing-tips I would probably have tripped over. The man had style. It just wasn't anybody else's.

"Frank-san," he said, sticking out a hand. He wore leather fingerless gloves, as though he'd sped to the Tom and Mary in a Formula One race car. He pulled me over to the bar and introduced me to Kenji, who wore black trousers and a blinding-white shirt with sleeves rolled to just below the elbow. The rolls looked like they'd been tailored into the shirt.

"Kenji, ah, he speak good English. He gonna explain rule."

The place was full, and it felt like every customer was watching. My stomach did a rollover.

"It's simple," said Kenji. He filled a lacquered tray with drinks as he talked. "Three sets, two breaks, you keep the tips. We got regulars—they know jazz. Goto-san says you know jazz."

"Lots," I said. Kenji's hands never stopped moving.

"Goto-san wants the old songs. You play them your way. You get requests for anything else, okay. Customer is God. We like it, you can stay."

"So this is just a trial."

"We don't like it, back to piano lessons for rich Japanese ladies."

I didn't care for Kenji or his pencil mustache. Goto watched us intently, his big lower lip thrust forward and his head turning from side to side. He might not have understood everything, but he wasn't giving up control.

"He'll like it," I said.

"Ten thousand yen a night." He reached under the counter and handed me a single banknote.

I was paying the Australian guy a twelve hundred dollars a month for his microscopic apartment. Kenji had just given me $106, which wouldn't go far. He shrugged.

"I told you. Tips are yours." He said something to Goto in Japanese. Goto said, "Hah!" and clapped me on the shoulder. He grabbed a drink off Kenji's tray and pushed me toward the piano. I felt like the spaniel that's lost a pissing contest with a couple of Dobermans.

But I could play piano, and they couldn't. I sat down beneath a limpet-shaped lampshade, and suddenly Kenji and his boss were on the other end of the transaction. I started with "My Funny Valentine" for old times' sake, and I played right through my first break. By the time I finally stood up again, there were three of those nice ten-thousand-yen notes on the polished black surface of the music desk. Somebody liked me.

When I finally walked over to the bar, Kenji's cuffs were as immaculate as ever and his hands were still moving. He gave me a tiny head duck and slid a cold glass of beer across the bar, along with two skewers of *yakitori*.

"So, not too awful?" I said.

Kenji went back to his wall of bottles. It was my turn to shrug. Goto was nowhere to be seen, which was fine with me. I finished the beer, wolfed the grilled chicken and went back to play my last set. I was deep into a long riff on the old standard "The Man I Love" when I realized there were people beside me. A quick look— three people, Goto in the middle, wearing a blissed-out expression and an alcohol buzz. The guys on either side of him wore identical black suits and stone faces. The only thing different about them was their hair. One had lots of it, slicked back in fifties greaser style. The other man's hair was cut short, but it took off from a low forehead and shelved up and back at a steep angle. His face looked like the business end of a chisel. The two of them oozed testosterone and cheap cologne.

Goto belched. His breath was sweet with alcohol. His friends watched while he pulled banknotes from a gold money clip and placed them on top of the others. This was heady stuff. It beat staying at home and watching *The Eating Championship* on TV. I was on top of the world.

Within a couple of weeks, I'd settled into a routine. I still had my students, but now I also played five nights a week. For four of those I just walked from my closet-sized apartment through the park to the Tom and Mary. But every Wednesday, after Akiko's lesson, I'd catch the 8:03 train back to Kichijoji.

That was how I met the Woman on the Train.

The Woman on the Train

Habit and coincidence are funny things. My chances of running into Kaz Nakamura were essentially zero—but now I was starting to see the same woman every week. It was the schedule, of course— she had hers and I had mine, and they happened to coincide. So it wasn't random at all. But it still unnerved me, because the first time I saw the Woman on the Train I half hoped I'd never see her again. I might not be able to control myself.

But then I did see her again. And again. After a couple of weeks, I was as well trained as a show dog. As soon as I saw the pink sign that said *Keio Railway Line*, my heart began to pound. Now it was Wednesday again, and the Woman on the Train was right across from me.

I tried to concentrate on my *Japan Times*. We were into July, and Tokyo was hot and bothered. Even in hyper-polite Japan, tempers were fraying, and these days you could sum it up in one acronym: TEPCO. The Tokyo Electric Power Company was responsible for the radioactive mess in Fukushima. According to the *Times*, TEPCO's top brass were apologizing 24/7. But the truth was, they couldn't control what was going on at their nuclear site.

Planes bombed the reactors with seawater to cool them. Evacuations were botched and secret meetings held. Radioactivity seeped into the ocean. Here in sweltering Tokyo, housewives might be freaking out over radioactive radishes, but the big story was the Fukushima Fifty. It was a group of heroes who had pledged to fix the reactors or die trying.

Or so the newspapers said.

It was almost enough to distract me from the Woman on the Train. As usual, she didn't quite fit. The other women were dolled up in high-heeled boots and Gucci bags. But this one wore jeans and carried a simple leather shoulder bag. Her hair wasn't teased or tinted. It simply framed a long straight nose, a mole at one corner of the mouth. Her eyes were slightly puffy, as though she never got quite enough sleep. What endeared her to me most was her hands. They were large and capable-looking, hands that could do more than twiddle the buttons of a smartphone. This woman will stay beautiful, I thought. She'll keep smiling, and she'll let her hair go gray, and we'll live happily ever after.

Infatuation—you've got to love it.

But there was something even more distracting in that railway car—someone was coughing. Japanese people keep their germs to themselves, behind white surgical masks. All you see is a pair of watery eyes. But a guy near the exit was coughing, weakly and annoyingly, like a screen door banging in the wind. He wasn't wearing a mask.

He was a *gaijin* like me. Pale, probably in his twenties, in a dirty overcoat clutched around his stubbled chin. His other arm clung to the metal handgrip as though he was afraid of being washed away. Each time he coughed, he ducked his mouth inside his coat. There were drops in his scraggly beard. The guy wasn't coughing. He was vomiting.

The train was full, even at this hour. Every seat was taken except for a little buffer zone around the sick man. Most of the passengers had their heads down over a smartphone or a comic book. Some were bolt upright but asleep. One young businessman in tight pinstriped trousers stared into some invisible distance. The dribbling *gaijin* might as well have been invisible too. He was a human Fukushima having his own meltdown. He crept out at Kugayama Station. I watched him sink to his knees on the platform.

Two stops later, the Woman on the Train rose to leave. I concentrated on a headline that said, *TEPCO Reassures Public About Radiation Leaks*. Suddenly the newspaper shook in my face.

"This is not correct," the woman said. She smacked the newspaper again. The train dove underground and slowed, and she staggered a little. "They are not truthful."

It was an astonishing outburst from a stranger. The train stopped opposite a huge billboard advertising the giant Mitsukoshi department store. A perky young woman perched on a shiny mound of merchandise. *You are what you buy*, it read. I watched the Woman on the Train disappear in the throng and I thought, There goes one who isn't. And she speaks English!

The week passed quickly. The next time I saw her, she handed me a leaflet across the aisle of the train. There was a public protest that weekend. "You maybe should come," she said. When she got off the train I jumped off and followed, hurrying past the billboard and catching up with her at street level. A woman in a pink raincoat bowed and handed me a packet of tissues. The Woman on the Train turned, as though she'd known all along I was huffing along behind her.

"Do you like jazz?" I said. I handed her my Tom and Mary business card, Japanese-style, with both hands and an awkward bow. She looked at it gravely.

"Sometimes," she said.

Pachinko

Her name was Momo, and she worked in a pastry shop in Shibuya. The rally she sent me to didn't feature rock throwing and riot police. But it was huge. Even the police put the numbers at more than a hundred thousand—a lot of people to be crammed into Meiji Park on a sweltering July day. I circulated around the edge of a sea of chanting people in yellow vests and gas masks. People beat drums and waved yellow No Nukes signs. Various speakers whipped up the crowd, including a tattooed ex-stripper turned environmentalist. Although Japanese people tend to have a lot of faith in routine, this event was anything but.

My own routines continued. My gigs at the Tom and Mary got better. My students plodded on. Every week Mrs. Ogawa looked a little more heat-flushed. Akiko turned on the air-conditioning, and I began to pack a sweater to the lesson. Akiko became icier too, as though I had committed a blunder so grave you couldn't even acknowledge it. She never mentioned Mr. Goto.

But Goto and his customers at the Tom and Mary were doing good things for my bottom line. One night the stars aligned. I hit my stride and never lost it. Thousand-yen tips settled on my piano like the autumn leaves in Inokashira Park. Even Kenji looked on the verge of smiling. I've made it, I thought. It was a tiny triumph, my shaky start as a real musician in one of the world's toughest markets. Next up was a walk through the deserted park and the sweet dive onto my futon. Perfection.

And that should have been that, one of life's little highs that we never get enough of. But it wasn't. I looked up, and there was Momo.

She was alone at a table along the wall. I'd given her my business card and gone to the protest rally. We'd even taken to nodding to each other on the 8:03 from Shibuya, but I'd never expected to see her here. And in two seconds I went on full alert. It was like accelerating for a green light and having it suddenly turn red. Because Momo wasn't gazing adoringly in my direction or swaying happily over a forest of empties. She was staring at the back of Goto's head. I could almost see the bull's-eye.

I managed to get Oscar Peterson's "Night Train" safely into the station, and by the time I looked up again, Momo was gone. I slipped past Goto and his friends at the bar and out into the warm night. Momo was waiting. The smile I looked forward to every Wednesday on the train wasn't in evidence. She fell into step beside me. When we reached the end of the lane and turned down toward the park, she stayed with me, so close I could smell her perfume.

We started down the broad steps that led to the park. Halfway down, she tugged at my elbow and got in front of me. She had to look up to meet my eyes.

"They are bad men," she said. Her eyes never left mine.

"Who?"

"You know. Goto." She spat the name out like a rotten oyster.

I was tired. My shoulders hurt. Suddenly I just wanted to be home in bed. "How do you know about Goto?" I said.

Momo opened the leather bag I'd always admired on the train. She pulled out a wallet and extracted a snapshot. A young man, maybe twenty. Jacket and tie, black glasses, serious expression.

"My brother," Momo said. "His name was Ryu." She took a long, wavering breath. "Goto killed him."

I felt like the shiny steel ball caroming around inside a pachinko machine. There are lots of pachinko parlors in Japan. Each one is a garish, bonging, smoke-filled universe of pinball addicts hammering money into slots. The Japanese couldn't seem to get enough pachinko. And there was lots of money in it. I wouldn't have been surprised if Mr. Goto owned a couple of pachinko parlors.

Now here I was, pinballed in a single day from earnest, boring Mrs. Ogawa—*ping!*—to a mobster in my student's living room. And then, only a few days later, letting it all hang out in a subterranean piano bar—*pong!*— and pocketing five hundred bucks a night in tips. That alone would have been enough to make any sensible person consider taking a breather. But no, whoever was playing my machine had something else in store. I'd also developed a crush on someone I didn't know. Fair enough—Tokyo is full of attractive women. But this one was gazing up at me in the glow of a streetlight outside Inokashira Park at one in the morning. *Boinnng!* Now was definitely the time to hand back the picture of Momo's dead brother, hang up the Out of Order sign and take myself out of the game.

None of which, of course, I did.

The Fukushima Fifty

I stared stupidly at the kid's picture until Momo took it back. She linked her arm through mine and tugged me toward the park. "Do you want to hear?" she said.

Part of me knew even then that the right answer was, *What about that job at the pastry shop? Shouldn't you be getting some sleep?* But Momo felt good in the dark. Her head came up to my shoulder. It was just me and her and the cherry trees. Even the crows had gone to bed.

"Tell me all about it," I said.

"Ryu would be twenty-five now," Momo said. "Five years younger than me

But something happened to him. As a teen-ager. He became *hikikomori*. How do you say in English? Maybe stay-at-home boy. This is big problem in Japan, you know."

I didn't.

"Ryu stopped going school, all day in his room, never come out. I am finishing high school, I can't help. Nobody can help. My parents operate farm. It's very bad situation."

"Farm?"

"My family is from small village. It's hard life for them. Young people want to go Tokyo."

"Including you?"

Momo took her time answering. We walked along the edge of the artificial lake, where you could rent rowboats and churn through floating cherry blossoms. There were pedal boats too, in the shape of enormous white swans, and I could just make out a long row of them at the dock.

Their curved necks made them look like cobras ready to strike.

"I came here to look for Ryu," Momo finally said. "One day he was gone. We thought he would go Tokyo. So I became Tokyo Girl."

Inokashira Park was deserted. In a few hours it would be thronging with dog walkers and schoolgirls with furry pink animals dangling from their book bags. Commuters on bicycles would weave around babies and banjo players. The pedestrian mall outside the Tom and Mary would be a river of humanity. There were thirteen million people in Tokyo. How did you find one runaway kid?

"It took three years," Momo said, as though she had read my thoughts. "Just I keep trying. There are many places in Tokyo where homeless go. You don't see them."

I thought of the vomiting *gaijin* on the train. There, but invisible.

"Ryu was in one of these places. He looked not so good. But he's trying. Sometimes he let me bring him food. In winter, it's very cold here. But Ryu was getting better. Even he starts talking about getting a job. Then *jishin*."

She said the last word in a whisper. I leaned down.

"Earthquake," Momo said. "Fukushima. Everybody changed."

"Even in Tokyo?"

"Fukushima is not so far. We have many aftershock in Tokyo. And then there is reactor situation. Everybody is frightened. Everybody is angry."

That much I knew. I could still see the crowds in Meiji Park, the protesters' flags and radiation masks and megaphones.

"And then you lost him again," I said. We were halfway through the park now, and I was beginning to feel lost myself. At night, the pleasant and familiar became unfriendly.

The massive trees that provided such welcome shade during the day now seemed to enclose and threaten. Their twisted trunks became the looming creatures of nightmares. A ghostly pool of light floated toward us, and I jumped. But it was only a lone pedestrian, head bowed over a glowing smartphone.

"The *yakuza* took him. To Fukushima. I never saw Ryu again."

"The *yakuza*?" This was going too fast. "I thought *yakuza* were, like, small-time gangsters. Extortion, protection money, construction, that kind of thing." And piano bars, I thought. Maybe Momo didn't quite understand my English, but she got the message.

"Not now. Now *yakuza* are businessmen. No more cutting fingers off if you make mistake. Whatever you want, *yakuza* give you good price."

"But what does that have to do with your brother?"

"*Yakuza* provide people too. Especially for jobs nobody want. You remember Fukushima Fifty?"

Heroic workers struggle to contain runaway reactors? I did remember that. A newspaper story read on a crowded train. It seemed like another life now. Before Momo.

"Not only fifty. Many more. My brother one of Fukushima Fifty. Your boss sent him there."

We were nearing the border of the park. Now the path would follow the sluggish river to the next station, at Kugayama. There would be houses again now, with miniature front gardens and orange trees and the dusty park where the old men played *shogi*. I just wanted to sleep.

"Goto's not my boss," I said.

Momo squeezed my arm and pulled me to a stop. She looked up at me, half smiling.

"Did you know that Japanese boys used to capture crickets?" she said. "They keep them as little pets, in cages."

"I didn't know that." Where was this going?

Momo laughed. "Now you are Goto's cricket."

"Only until I quit."

Momo pulled me ahead. We were under streetlights again, and they lit the overhanging trees from beneath. The ghostly branches spanned the river. In a few minutes we would pass the Foot Park shoe store and the Snack Bohème bar with the neon sign that read *Whiskey and Music*. And then I'd be home.

"Ryu couldn't quit the job Goto gave him," Momo finally said. "Neither can you."

We left the river and passed a tidy row of locked commuter bicycles outside the train station. The tracks ran twenty feet from my little block of bachelor apartments.

The trains would rattle the clothes hanger on my balcony and cover my shirts with dust.

"Thank you for listening my story," Momo said. She stood on tiptoe, brushed my cheek with her lips, then ran into the station. Fast but effective.

Maybe I should have asked Momo how she knew her brother was dead. But my rational self seemed to have run away with her.

Earthquake

I didn't sleep well that night—what was left of it. It wasn't the trains that kept me awake, or the after-buzz of late-night performing. I'd played in Kaz Nakamura's bar in Nanaimo four nights a week for three years before Kaz disappeared. I knew how to hit the pillow, switch off and get six solid hours.

But in all that time, I hadn't exactly lived a life of romantic excess. For a guy who had tuned pianos all day, taken a nap and then played all night, the chances of hooking up with the right woman were slim.

But I was in a city of thirteen million now. Statistically, there were 162 times the number of women in Tokyo than there were in Nanaimo. And you had to be living under a rock not to realize that many Japanese women found Western men attractive. I'd seen plenty of giddy, glamorous girls clinging to lumbering Australians and Americans. Now maybe I was part of the pool. Still—a couple of weeks fantasizing about a woman on a train, and suddenly she's kissing me under a streetlight? It was too easy.

That was what was keeping me awake. Kisses didn't normally land on me quite that easily. Momo's had been more of a peck than a kiss, but it had still felt good. Replaying it in the eerie silence before the trains started rattling past my window had been good for an hour or so of insomnia. Dissecting everything she'd told me about her brother's tragedy and the business practices of my new employer had taken care of the rest. Eventually I decided to dwell on the kiss rather than the story. I finally drifted off to the sound of my neighbor coughing through the wall.

Waking up was one of those experiences that reminds you not to take anything for granted in Japan. Two things registered. First, there was natural light leaking through the grimy blind, so it had to be dawn. Second, my bed was moving. Not just my bed—the whole floor, the whole room, probably the whole building, was swaying. It was like lying on an air mattress in a swimming pool when the fat guy jumps in. The weirdest thing was the silence. No crashes, no creaks, not even the sound of a picture falling off the wall. Not that I had any pictures.

The earthquake lasted a minute or so, long enough to make me wonder whether it was ever going to stop. Another aftershock from the big one in Fukushima? I knew that if I flipped on the TV, a serious-looking lady would already be standing in front of a map of Japan. A pulsing red dot would tell us the location and how bad it was. For weeks the coastline between Tokyo and Fukushima had been a string of red lights. I waited this one out, but I got the message: if you think you've got everything figured out, think again.

At least I was smart enough to do a little research on Mr. Goto. When my room stopped swimming, I fried two eggs, grilled a halved baguette, opened a tub of excellent yogurt and made coffee. Food was cheap in Japan, and always startlingly fresh. I turned on my laptop.

There was plenty to read, in English, on Akiko's jazz-loving sugar daddy. Mr. Goto was something of a celebrity, if you followed the ups and downs of what some people called the Japanese Mafia—the *yakuza*.

The missing finger meant he was old-school. In those days, having a digit chopped off was the price you paid for missteps on your climb up the ladder. For a guy in his sixties, as Goto seemed to be, today's young *yakuza* must have seemed spineless and soft. No tattoos, and their intact fingers in legitimate businesses, just like the mob in North America. Technically, being a *yakuza* wasn't even illegal.

Goto seemed to be high up in one of the three major *yakuza* "families" in Tokyo. It made sense that he'd have his hand in a bar or two, and that he could indulge his fondness for jazz and young women. So yes, Goto was a bad guy, but I had known that the moment he stepped into Akiko's music lesson. Unfortunately, there wasn't anything helpful on the responsibilities of a lowly employee like me. Momo's warning about my being somehow bound to Akiko's protector was going to have to wait to be proved valid.

She had been right, though, about *yakuza* involvement in Fukushima. The story about her brother and others being scooped off the street and put to work in the nuclear reactor looked true. And it wasn't just Western reporters and bloggers with an agenda who were sounding the alarm. There were plenty of Japanese sources too, one of them writing in tolerable English. He had actually gotten himself sent into the reactors and sneaked his stories out. The heroic Fukushima Fifty had been a lot more than fifty, and most of them had come from the lowest level of Japanese society. The final link wasn't a pleasant one. TEPCO, the all-powerful electric utility, had subcontracted the hiring of these unfortunate men to the *yakuza*.

Or so the Internet told me. How was I to judge? Hiring workers was a perfectly legal thing to do. The way the *yakuza* put it, they were doing a public service. And if Momo was right, that meant you had to give Goto some credit. The thing is, was she right?

They say that Japan's crowded society functions smoothly because all Japanese learn, right from the start, how to keep their real feelings behind a mask. Deception is a survival skill. I'd seen the TEPCO top brass covering their asses on TV, and I seemed to be working for a Tokyo gangster who had a place in Japanese society. As far as I was concerned, such people were unlikable, dishonest, possibly even evil. Against that, Momo had felt good on my arm, and I could still feel that almost-kiss. I decided to go with what felt good.

A train jammed with commuters thundered past my apartment, and the last of my coffee trembled in its cup. The trains were coming every five minutes or so now, peak commuter timing. I'd overslept. Today was Wednesday, so I'd be spending some serious time on the train myself.

I had Mrs. Ogawa at ten, then Goto's enigmatic girlfriend. After that, if there were no more aftershocks to throw the trains off schedule, I would see Momo again on the 8:03 out of Shibuya. I couldn't wait.

No Comment

Mrs. Ogawa didn't seem bothered by the tremor that had shaken me awake. *"Chiisai! Chiisai!"* she said, smiling and bobbing. Just a little one! She held her palms a few inches apart, in case I hadn't gotten the message. She was in good form all round, acing the first page of *Clair de Lune*. She even managed some real emotion where Debussy's directions are to slow down and savor the moment. I gave her a thumbs-up. She blushed.

On the street, though, Tokyo seemed twitchy. And once I began my long train journey to Akiko's house, the mood turned downright dark. Maybe the aftershocks and the rationed water were getting to people. Tokyoites on trains were reserved at the best of times. No conversation, no eye contact, much twiddling of cell phones. But today people were even stonier than usual. I was glad to escape, find my noodle shop and lose myself in steam and cigarette smoke.

When I got to Akiko's house, even her fish seemed out of sorts, sliding behind an overhanging rock and ignoring the possibility of food I represented. Something else was different—there was another car shoehorned in behind Akiko's Lexus. There was no way Akiko could have gotten out. Whoever he was, politeness wasn't his strong suit.

I hesitated at the polished cypress door. Should I walk away? Come back later? But Akiko was Japanese, too polite not to keep her appointment. I pushed the button.

Usually, there was a long delay before the door swung silently open, as though

Akiko had to float down from some other part of her house. This time it was different. I heard a muffled thump. Then a door slammed and a man walked through the carport. He was carrying a briefcase, not as fancy as the crocodile one Goto had, but thick enough to carry a substantial stash of—what? Money? Drugs? He saw me, turned, bowed slightly and got unhurriedly into his car. The man was stocky, suited and with a strangely shaped head. The last time I'd seen him, he'd been watching his boss tip me for my rendition of "The Lady Is a Tramp." Chisel Face. Goto's man.

Then the front door opened.

The lesson that followed took awkwardness to new heights. Akiko didn't look at me once. And after I caught a glimpse of the goose egg welling up on her smooth forehead, I didn't catch her eye either. Her wrists, when she extended them over the keys, were raw and red. Her hair, which was normally in a long braid, looked as though it had been used as a mop, and the neckline of her T-shirt was loopy and stretched. The shirt had sparkles on the front, two cats embracing.

"Nice," I said, when she'd finished the piece. And it was, too. She'd worked hard. "Are you okay?"

She pointed to a spot in the music. "Left hand is still difficult."

I knew that assaults on women were still under-reported in Japan, but the person next to me had been tossed around like a doll. "Shouldn't you call the police?" I said. Akiko gave the slightest of sighs and tapped the page again. The manicured fingernail was broken off. I sneaked a look at her face. It was as stony as a TEPCO boss's. I was never going to lift that mask.

"Okay. Let's see if a different fingering works." I picked up a pencil from the music desk and wrote one in. Then we tiptoed through the rest of the hour. When I left she didn't follow me to the door. She just sat staring at the dense cluster of notes on the music score, as though there might be some safety there for her. "Good luck," I said, like an idiot.

Outside, the koi were still in hiding. What passes for twilight in Tokyo had started to fall. I walked back to the station in a haze of lingering heat, car exhaust and confusion. Akiko lived in a neighborhood so classy that even the manhole covers were cast in an elegant cherry-blossom motif. Yet she refused to acknowledge that large men kept feeding her a diet of money and punches. She was becoming toxic for me.

The need to see Momo was suddenly acute, as though she represented everything Akiko didn't. By the time the 8:03 pulled in, I'd decided. Akiko was bad news. If Momo was sitting where she usually did, I'd make her my ticket to happiness.

The doors sighed open. A tide of passengers flowed out onto the platform. And there she was.

Dear Frank

I took a seat across from Momo, between a schoolgirl and a businessman. Both could have been emblems of modern Japan. The girl wore a blazer and a pleated plaid skirt that revealed blotchy knees. She clutched a regulation leather satchel. The man was in a black suit, tie askew. Both were sound asleep, their lowered heads waving with the movement of the train. Like seaweed in a current. Momo paid no attention to anyone, including me. Her big hands held some kind of book. Russian novel? A collection of cake recipes? I had no way of knowing. Japanese books all looked the same to me, a splash of letters on the cover but rarely a picture. She turned another page, left to right. I concentrated on the advertisements for cosmetics that ran above her head.

The schoolgirl came suddenly alive, snuck a look at me, jumped to her feet and walked off the train. At the next stop Momo stood up and crossed to the exit. When the doors parted, she reached over the sleeping businessman, handed me a note and vanished. She didn't look back.

In my experience, people sometimes write notes when they don't want to deliver bad news in person. And Japanese people are legendary for finding ways not to say no. I knew what would be in this letter. *Sayonara*, Frank, and please consider taking a different train on Wednesdays.

The businessman gave a sudden snort, adjusted his tie and got to his feet. It was my stop too, and for some reason I was hungry again. If I had to get bad news, I wanted to be surrounded by food and alcohol and the anonymity of a crowded restaurant. I saw the telltale red paper lanterns of a ramen shop and ducked in. There was gray lino on the floor, and the restaurant shook as a train ran overhead. I downed half an Asahi beer and opened Momo's letter.

Dear Frank-san, Momo had written. *Thank you for lovely time in Inokashira Park. Is such romantic place, don't you think?* I finished my beer and motioned for another one. *I like to see you again, but your apartment is dangerous.* Dangerous? True, the bathroom was the size of a phone booth, and the trains ran twenty feet from the window. But dangerous? Maybe she just meant thin-walled and smelly. I read on. *Please meet me next Sunday night at hotel Fifteen Love in Shibuya. Ten o'clock. It is up hill, across street from Joyful.* Beneath the writing was a deft drawing of a man bent over a piano keyboard. A woman perched on the end of the piano, legs crossed at the ankle. A stream of hearts flowed from her head to his.

I shoveled steaming noodles into my mouth. Shibuya was a huge district, but Momo had given me a clue. Up the hill? Tokyo was flat, so a hill would stand out. Fifteen Love seemed an odd name for a hotel, so that would be unique too. I had three days to solve the puzzle of its exact location.

The other puzzle never occurred to me until much later. How did Momo know Sunday was my night off?

By the time Sunday evening came around, I had dreamed up enough date scenarios to fill a writer's notebook. None of them, I'm ashamed to say, involved tragically deceased younger brothers. I got to Shibuya two hours early. The area around the station was an all-out assault of neon and three-story video screens, but I soon found the hill. The Fifteen Love was a nondescript building in an alley of taverns and adult stores. One of the stores was called Joyful.

I picked at a grilled mackerel in one of the taverns. Then I spent an hour nursing an espresso back at the train station. I visited the washroom. I was nervous. It had been a long time since I'd had a real date. Finally, it was time to walk back up the hill.

The Fifteen Love was surrounded by scooters and motorcycles and bicycles stashed under eaves and awnings. Momo was standing in front of a small sign that advertised the hotel's rates. There were two categories: rest and stay. Another puzzle. There was so much about this country I didn't understand. Especially its people. As a foreigner, was I treated the way a Japanese person would be? I seriously doubted it, and Momo proceeded to prove it.

She took my arm and grinned up at me. "You know love hotel?"

Discretion

I had, in fact, heard of love hotels. They were places for short-stay sex, useful in a country where privacy was hard to find. If the Fifteen Love was a love hotel, we'd crossed some threshold I wasn't aware of. Momo tugged me through the door into a lobby that reminded me of a McDonald's back home. A grid of illuminated pictures covered one wall, each with a name and a price. But they weren't pictures of donuts and coffees.

And there was nobody to take your order, only a neatly lettered, framed sign. It said, *The visitor who cannot speak Japanese withholds entrance into a room. I am sorry.*

"Never mind that," Momo said. "You are with me. You like this one?" She pointed to an image of pink and fluffiness, a roomful of stuffed toys and mirrors. *Hello Kitty*, the label said. A life-size stuffed cat wore a leather garter belt. "Maybe not," I said. The next one was Disney-themed, with a leering Mickey Mouse painted on the ceiling. Next was the Bad Girl room. It featured a mini classroom with table, school desk, blackboard and a convenient bed for naps. A pair of leather wrist restraints hung from crossed wooden beams.

"Occupied," said Momo, pointing to a small red light in one corner of the display. "Very popular, I think."

I cleared my throat. "I'm kind of a traditionalist," I said. My mental image of what those businessmen on the trains were dreaming about was getting rapidly revised. "How about this one?" I pointed to a room where two walls were covered by immense blowups of traditional Japanese erotic woodblock prints. The couples were in postures that looked more like yoga poses than sex, but at least they were managing without handcuffs. "I always liked the classics," I said.

Momo punched *Rest* on the screen. "Room is open now," she said. "We pay later." I followed her down a soothingly lit hallway to the elevator. Next to it was another lighted display, this one of women's costumes. There were dozens of them, each model smiling cheerfully. Schoolgirl, nurse, flight attendant, office worker. One young lady beamed from inside a full kimono. The only flesh visible was her face and hands.

"We don't need," said Momo. She pulled me into the elevator, and we headed up toward my first date in Japan.

As dates go, my "rest" in the Fifteen Love with Momo went quickly to the top of an admittedly modest heap. For one thing, there was no tiptoeing around the issue of sex. We were surrounded by life-size images of sixteenth-century Japanese maidens being ravished by men with their hair in a topknot. A couple of them were doing it in a wooden hot tub. We weren't expected to disappoint them.

For another thing, sex for Momo seemed perfectly natural. The Fifteen Love had its own version of the samurai's hot tub, with jets, bubbles, black lights and a shelf of lotions and oils. Momo had a rare ability to communicate exactly what she wanted from me, to ask me what I liked and to make both happen. She gave me hints and giggled when I took them. After two hours under the watchful eye of the couples on the walls, thoughts of *yakuza* and dead brothers had been obliterated. I was tired, happy and hungry

We still have to pay," Momo said. We were both dressed again. I felt out of place amid the tangled sheets and the still-churning hot tub. "Watch." Momo unscrewed the top of a metal tube that curved out of the electronic command center near the head of the bed. She inserted a roll of banknotes, recapped the tube and pushed a button. There was a *whoosh*. "Old style," she said. "Very Japanese." Another *whoosh*, a faint *ding* and Momo unscrewed the top again and extracted a single bill. "Change," she said.

I'd heard that Japan was a society where discretion was what kept millions of people from rubbing each other raw. Now I knew what discretion was. The door clunked electronically open. We'd been locked in the whole time.

"I'm hungry," Momo said.

"I know a place," I said. We rode the elevator down and walked back up the narrow street. It was still all systems go in the bars and clubs and restaurants.

Momo clung to my arm, and I tried to keep my feet on the ground. Somehow we navigated back to the little restaurant where I'd left a grilled mackerel half eaten two hours earlier. We ordered the same, this time with pork dumplings that exploded in my mouth and battered octopus balls with mustard. The hot sake had bits of grilled fish fin floating in it. It tasted smoky and superb, and I got quickly drunk. We wolfed the food and gave ourselves over to the smells and shouts of a Japanese tavern in full swing.

Finally, Momo folded her paper napkin into a wedge. She rested her chopsticks across it. Then she took my elbow in both hands. She leaned into my shoulder and spoke into my sauce-spattered shirt. I had to lower my head to hear her.

"Can I ask question?" she said.

Hello Sunshine

"**A**m I prettier than Akiko-san?"

I hadn't seen that one coming. "My student?"

"Unh." Momo snuggled a little closer into my chest.

"How could you know about Akiko?"

Momo laughed. "Everyone knows who is Goto's mistress. Akiko-san is not only one. But, I think, she is only one who takes piano lessons." Another squeeze. "From a such sweet *gaijin*."

They say that really big cities are just a collection of towns. Tokyo obviously qualified, and Momo and I were the proof.

We'd gone from sharing a train car to cuddling on barstools and discussing my piano students. I gave her an answering squeeze. "You and Akiko? Not even in the same league. Akiko the icicle, I call her."

"Unh?"

"It's like a long, hanging spear of ice. Sometimes it drops on your head."

Momo digested this information. It seemed to satisfy her. Then she said, "Can I ask favor?"

Japanese taverns are loud places. The cooks and the servers yell orders back and forth. They greet and thank their customers, bang woks and plunge various forms of protein into seething oil. Alarm bells, especially the tiny internal ones, are hard to hear in a Japanese tavern at one in the morning. At least, that's my excuse.

"A favor? Why not?" Already I was thinking of next Sunday.

"Only if it's okay with you," Momo said. She did an endearing sideways thing with her lower lip.

"Of course it's okay. What's the favor?"

"Goto-san keeps an account book. But it's not money. It's a list of names, dates, ages. Places."

I yawned. Now that I'd eaten, I suddenly felt exhausted. "An account book," I said. "Not too surprising. What's the favor?"

Momo dropped my arm and began to doodle in a puddle of soya sauce. "This one has names of all men his company sold to TEPCO. For work in reactor."

"The Fukushima Fifty?"

"And Ryu, I think. I have to know. All I need is, see this list." She seized my arm again. "I need to know. My parents need to know. Can you help us?"

"You want me to steal an account book from a *yakuza* boss."

"No, no, not steal. Just—just only if you see it. Then you can tell me. That man, I think he killed my brother." She wiped up the spilled sauce and crumpled the napkin. "I need to know," she said again. Her voice had gotten small, and she lowered her head. *"O-negai shimasu."* Please.

What harm could it do? People left things lying around. Maybe I would spot the ledger, maybe I wouldn't. Maybe Goto carried it around in his precious crocodile briefcase. She wasn't asking me to steal it.

"How will I recognize it?" I said. Momo took a pen out of her bag and wrote two characters on the back of the bill for our food. Squiggles and dots. They meant nothing to me, but I could recognize them if I saw them again. I pulled out some money for the food and put the bill in my wallet.

"I'll do my best," I said.

Momo pulled my head down and brushed my ear with her lips. She bit gently. "Next Sunday," she whispered.

When I got back to my apartment, my legs had turned to lead and my memory had turned selective. Account books and dead brothers were no match for flavored sake and a nip on the ear. I crept into the phone-booth-sized shower and stood under the hot water, washing off scented oils from the Fifteen Love. By the time I whipped the covers off my bed, I was half asleep. But what I uncovered woke me up fast.

There was a fish in my bed. And not just any fish. Sunshine, Akiko's favorite koi, had been opened from gills to tail, the guts artfully arranged on the sheet. Heart, liver, pearly coils of intestine, the shiny, deflated balloon of the swim bladder. And two slender white fingers of the testes, so Akiko had been right. Sunshine was a boy. His insides were dusted with golden scales. If a fish could commit *hara-kiri*, it would want to look like this, artful and obscene.

Sunshine's eyes were clouded, and he was starting to smell. I grabbed the edges of the sheet and drew it around him. Then I rolled everything into a bloody white package and shoved it into the refrigerator next to a four-pack of Asahi. But Sunshine's juices had seeped into the mattress. My bed smelled like the Tsukiji fish market at the end of a long day.

I pulled the blanket off, curled up on the floor and tried to sleep. The light beside my bed was still on, and I wasn't about to turn it off. And the questions kept coming at me like an army of unkillable zombies. None of the answers made me feel any better.

Who had done this? Someone with a sharp knife, a taste for violence and a sense of its formalities. Goto didn't need to do this kind of work, but he had men in suits and cheap cologne who would. Why was easily answered. This was obviously a warning. But why *me*? And why now? True, I'd seen a well-dressed thug come out of Akiko's house, but how did that make me a threat? If Goto didn't want me around his girlfriend, all he had to do was tell her to stop the lessons. The last time I'd seen the man, he was shelling out ten-thousand-yen notes each time I played one of his favorites. Maybe he was just the kind of person who liked to spread the hurt around. And maybe this was why Momo had called my apartment dangerous.

I'd spent the entire evening hidden away in a love hotel, a place where discretion was the entire point. Momo and her determination to get to the bottom of her brother's death couldn't possibly have anything to do with Sunshine's. No, the only connection I had to anyone who got off on disemboweling pet fish was Akiko. I tried to imagine a man in a hot suit chasing a big fish around with a net. Did he club it to death first? Did he put the corpse in his trunk, in true gangster style? Did he ransack Akiko's house for one of my business cards to get my address, or did he just beat it out of her?

That was as far as I had gotten when the first trains began to run at five in the morning. Akiko would either cancel her lessons, or she wouldn't. Either way, it was about her, not me. Sunshine was her favorite, not mine. I would wait and see and count the days until next Wednesday. I pulled the fishy blanket around my shoulders. I concentrated on how I'd felt when Momo had emerged from the shower and stepped into the churning purple of the marble hot tub. Finally I drifted off.

The Boss

For the next few days, Japan was all about the nuclear reactors in Fukushima. The local media featured apologizing officials and the unimaginable task of cleaning up after a disaster that had turned thousands into refugees. Every one of them had to be sheltered, fed, doctored and reassured. Japan had its hands full. The country also had to deal with Western nations who wouldn't stop pointing out that TEPCO had dropped the ball from the moment seawater got into the control rooms. North Americans were sending in donations while worrying about contaminated debris washing up on their own beaches.

With this kind of attention, Japan was going to do whatever it took to clean those reactors up. Even if it meant subcontracting the hiring of suicide squads to the *yakuza*. The *Japan Times* carried an article on key members of the Tokyo *yakuza*, and their role in "helping" deal with the crisis. That made me feel better. If Goto had the spotlight on him, maybe he'd back off on the girlfriend bashing and the fish killing.

But when I approached Akiko's front door on Wednesday, the little speech I had ready, about Sunshine and his stomach contents and my bed, went out the window. Because there were still two koi circling in Akiko's pond. And one of them was a deep, burnished gold. The door opened silently, and Akiko joined me. She was wearing sunglasses so large they covered a third of her face. We watched the two fish nibble at algae growing on the rocks.

"Sunshine is feeling much better now," Akiko said. She drew off the sunglasses and led me inside. When she sat down at the piano I saw that one eye was puffy, even under a heavy layer of makeup. If she wasn't going to acknowledge Sunshine's disappearance and reincarnation, neither was I. She sat erect as a grade-schooler and played through her Chopin prelude better than any student of mine had ever done. Something—grief, resignation, maybe even anger—was being channeled into this music. There was no need for me to plead for more emotion now.

"Again, please," I said. I got up and made a slow circle of the piano as she played, and the music was even better this time. Do it, I told myself. Get it over with. I ran my eyes quickly over all the surfaces in the room, although there weren't many. A chair, an ebony table with a statue of a Chinese courtesan carved from an elephant tusk, which had to be a pointed gift from Goto. Nowhere for even a speck of dust, let alone Momo's mysterious account book. But I'd looked. I'd done my duty. When I heard a door open, I clasped my hands behind my back, music-teacher style, and kept moving.

"Frank." Goto clapped me on the shoulder with one hand and held on to the crocodile briefcase in the other. "Good?" he said, gesturing at his girlfriend's back. Akiko played on. These people had taken discretion to new levels. I was out of my depth.

"Remarkably good," I said. "All things considered." Goto whacked me on the back again and headed off into another room, leaving a vapor trail of Dunhill. How many businesses did he have his fingers in? Bars and human trafficking, I already knew. What about prostitution? Maybe a love hotel or two? Maybe the ledger was in the valise, maybe it was under Akiko's bed. I didn't care. I couldn't wait for the lesson to end. I complimented Akiko, accepted my cash and hurried past the reborn Sunshine into the street.

After Akiko's air-conditioned cell, the pavement threw off heat like a griddle. A sailor-suited teenager on a bicycle swerved around me, and I staggered into a vending machine. It featured a picture of the actor Tommy Lee Jones glaring at a selection of Boss canned coffees. I bought an iced latte, but it didn't seem to make him any happier. He was frowning all the way to the bank.

My unhappiness was different. Unlike Mr. Jones, I actually lived in Japan. I even worked there. My problem was that, even if I learned the language properly, I would never be anything but a visitor. I would never know what was going on right under my nose.

On the plus side, the food was spectacular and people were polite. My success at the Tom and Mary was a powerful antidote to being a nobody back home. Here, I could be a somebody and a nobody at the same time. The nobody was invisible, but the somebody was making good money, tax free.

But Japanese people confused me. For example, one of my students refused to show any emotion when she played but burst into tears when she tried to imagine a full moon. Another student had rebuilt what had probably been a perfectly good face, allowed her boyfriend to rough her up and refused to cry—but she played beautifully. And her boyfriend—what was I to make of *him*? In the space of a few weeks he'd dropped a dream job in my lap, had one of his thugs put a deceased fish in my bed and slapped my back like an old friend the next day. Plus he'd caused the death of somebody's brother in a crippled nuclear reactor. And I was sleeping with that somebody.

I set off for the train station. Train stations were where the cheap restaurants were. I knew I could sit at a *kaiten-sushi* place—where chefs put color-coded plates of sushi on an endless conveyor belt—and gorge myself for the cost of a hamburger in Canada. Soon I would find myself across from Momo, awaiting her instructions for next Sunday. Momo might be my biggest Japanese puzzle, but she was also the only person I had actually connected with. When you're alone in a strange country, connection is hard to turn down. And if there was something about my new friend that didn't add up, the closer it came to Sunday night, the less I could concentrate on doing the math.

Better Than the First Time

The next Sunday when I met Momo in Shibuya, she wanted to eat first. That worked for me. Dinner gave me a chance to ask a few questions about those things that didn't quite add up.

Momo was waiting for me, but she wasn't in the restaurant when I first caught sight of her. There was a bookstore next door. It was one of those holes in the wall with geraniums outside and narrow aisles and an eccentric owner who wears a scarf at the height of summer. Momo had her back to me, bent slightly over one of the bargain tables outside. I got close enough to see she was leafing through a knitting book. Sweaters, scarves, hats—she turned the pages too quickly for me to tell. But it touched my heart, on top of my horniness and confusion. Not a good mix.

Momo turned, replaced the book and slotted herself under my shoulder as if we'd been a couple for years. "Hungry?" she asked.

"You can't imagine," I said.

I let her do the ordering. Two beers and an unstable pile of empty bowls later, I decided we were both mellow enough for me to raise the subject of her brother and the mysterious account book. Fun later; get this out of the way first.

"About Goto-san's ledger," I said. But that was as far as I got. Momo put a finger against my lips and shook her head.

"I'm so sorry," she said. "I never should tell you about my brother. Not your problem."

"Yeah, but…" Her finger tasted of soya and lemon. She shook her head slightly.

"I like you, Frank," she said. "Please don't worry about me. Okay?" She whispered the last word into my ear, then sat back and drained her glass. I decided to forget about the fish in my refrigerator. Fifteen Love, here we come.

It was even better than the first time. When Momo urged me to choose the same room we'd rented a week earlier, I wondered a bit, but the things she did once we got inside were all brand new. I prided myself on having a large repertoire of jazz tunes. Well, Momo seemed to have a pretty big repertoire in the lovemaking department. *Don't look a gift horse in the mouth,* Akiko had already cautioned me, and I wasn't about to start now. The busy samurai and his long-suffering lady looked down from the walls, and Momo played her tunes on me.

Somewhere between our first and second hop into the hot tub, my Westernness got the better of me. I began to feel guilty. The woman's brother was dead, but she was still treating me like royalty. Royalty felt good, but it had a way of making consequences melt away like the morning mist over Mount Fuji. I had to give her *something*.

"He always brings the same briefcase," I said.

"Unh?"

"Goto. He's always carrying that crocodile thing or whatever it is. Every time he comes to Akiko's house."

"Oh, Frank." There was a pause while Momo poured frangipani oil on my head. Then there was a longer pause. Finally, she said, "Probably that's money. *Yakuza* have a big problem with cash."

"You mean they have too much of it?"

"Too much, yes. So they have to, what do you say, wash money?"

"Launder it."

"Yes. But before laundry they have to hide. Goto must have safe."

"In Akiko's house? What if she opens it?"

Momo snorted. "Goto has safe in every girlfriend house. Of course, combination is secret."

Every girlfriend? The guy was at the age when such things began to slow down a little, wasn't he? I tried to imagine being one of his girlfriends. Accepting his gifts and knowing that somewhere, maybe even in your bedroom, there was a box of cash you could never open. It must be a constant reminder of who called the shots. For a man like Goto, money bought cars, sex, a new jazz pianist for one of your bars. Yet he still had to rub it in.

"Maybe the ledger is in the safe then."

"I don't think so. Many safes, only one book. If I am Goto-san, I keep this book with me always. Maybe even I sleep with it." Momo stepped into the hot tub and held out a hand. "Frankie. Forget this book."

I shook my head. What had Momo just said—*keep this book with me always*?

"That briefcase," I said. "He never lets go of it." I got back into the tub.

"Here is suggestion," Momo said, selecting another fragrant oil. "Next time Goto comes, just touch this bag. Maybe offer to help him. Then watch his face. In Japan, face is more important than words."

That sounded easy enough. Before Momo and I went back to creating a tsunami of our own in the Fifteen Love's hot tub, I resolved to try. It seemed the least I could do.

Crocodile Briefcase

It was another month before I finally got close to that crocodile briefcase. There were near misses. One week, Goto failed to show up. Another day, he hurried past the piano like a man desperate for the bathroom—or a safe to empty his booty into. Once, he actually arrived empty-handed and left dragging an enormous bag of golf clubs that looked like they'd never seen a blade of grass. The only time he stopped to talk, he kept his distance. It was all I could do to keep from staring at that damned reptilian thing in his hand.

I didn't really mind. The days went fast. The ones leading up to Sunday were Looking Forward to Momo days. The ones afterward were passed in dreamy, detailed replays. And through all the food and sex and growing affection, Momo never reminded me about my promise. I suppose she knew she didn't have to.

In the end, though, I did get something out of that briefcase. It just wasn't what I expected. One afternoon I was hovering near Akiko while she navigated a tricky section in a Mozart sonata. Goto arrived. He sank into the leather chair, laid the briefcase across his knees and snicked it open. No "Frank-san!" No slap on the back. Akiko didn't miss a beat, but my heart did.

I watched out of the corner of my eye. Goto took out an envelope, snapped the lid shut again, stood up and dropped the envelope on the chair. Akiko played on.

Then Goto caught me looking at him. That was when I knew I had a problem.

He gave me a look I'd never seen on him before. Or on any human. If a barracuda could smile, that's what it would look like. All this time, I thought I'd been watching Goto. But that smile told me it had been the other way around. Maybe he'd been reading my mind, something I was beginning to think Japanese people were pretty good at. If so, he hadn't liked what was written there. The look only lasted a heartbeat before Goto turned and left. But in that time, he stripped me bare.

Akiko finally finished. I hadn't really been listening. She put her hands in her lap, and her shoulders went down, as though someone had let the air out of her. "You may as well take it," she said.

"Take what?"

"The envelope. It's for you."

"How do you know?"

Akiko laughed. It wasn't a funny sound. "Poor Frank," she said. "You don't have any idea, do you? He gave it to you. You have to take it. Even if you don't, it won't change anything."

She got up like a sleepwalker, picked up the envelope and stuffed it into my shirt pocket. "Money is power, Frank." Akiko left the room and returned with her weekly lesson payment. She handed it to me formally, holding the bills with both hands and dipping her head. For a moment, she reminded me of stout, earnest Mrs. Ogawa.

"Goodbye, Frank," she said.

"Same time next week?"

"Please let yourself out." Akiko went back to the piano and began the Mozart again.

Something was very wrong. I half expected Chisel Face to be waiting for me beside the pond. Or a Mercedes with black-tinted windows to pull out behind me as

I walked to the train station. But neither of these things happened, and the good news was, it was Wednesday. I couldn't wait to see Momo, even if it was only for a wordless ride on a train. On Sunday, in the Fifteen Love, Momo would make it all go away.

I pulled out the envelope and headed toward the station, counting money as I walked. A hundred thousand yen, more than a thousand Canadian dollars. If Goto was angry with me, he had an odd way of showing it.

The next time Momo and I met in the Fifteen Love, I didn't mention the money or the look on Goto's face. When I tried to tell Momo I was still no closer to solving the puzzle of the crocodile briefcase, she just did that cute sideways thing with her lower lip. "Maybe next week," she said. "I trust you, Frank." She pulled my head down to hers.

That's how I wish I could remember her. If that night had been the last time I saw Momo, I'd have nothing but happy memories. But I did see her again, and that changed everything.

You Asked For It

It was my own fault. The next Wednesday, the first car on the 8:03 train was full. I dropped back to the second and squeezed on, but all I could think about was Momo sitting in the car ahead. This had never happened before. At Momo's stop I got off too, desperate for a glimpse of her. When I spotted her leather bag at the top of the stairs to the street, I made a big mistake. I followed her.

I felt guiltier with each step. But I didn't stop.

She didn't go far. Five minutes from the station, she entered a park. Near the gate, a severe-looking lady pulled on white gloves to wipe her spaniel's bottom and bag his droppings. The dog wore a frilly pink blouse. Momo leaned down to scratch it behind an ear. Then she kept walking. She was headed toward a playground next to a baseball diamond. This was the moment when I could have come to my senses, turned around, run. But I was in too deep. I kept following my Tokyo Girl.

Now Momo was talking to a stout, middle-aged woman in a cheap red windbreaker. The woman didn't have Momo's lovely shape. She looked like a fire hydrant. But she had the same nose, and when she gestured at something across the playground, I could see the same large hands. She handed Momo a beaten-looking blue backpack. Then they both turned and motioned at a child who was creeping up the incline of a seesaw. Hand straight out, fingers waving, the Japanese sign for *Come over here*.

The low sun was behind me, and the dusty playground managed to glow magically in the late-afternoon light. The team of young men practicing on the baseball diamond wore brilliant blue shirts. They darted after balls smacked high into the warm air, bolting like startled deer. I could see the little family clearly, but to them I must have been just an outline.

The boy was probably no more than four. He backed down the incline, turned and dawdled reluctantly back to Momo and her mother. The kid who reached out and took his mother's hand had a protruding lower lip and a scowl I could read from fifty feet away. All he needed was a miniature crocodile briefcase and a pair of Ray-Bans. Goto Jr.

I'd been had. It felt like a sucker punch, and I'd walked right into it. Momo was an ex-mistress of Goto's, maybe even Akiko's predecessor. She'd made the mistake of getting pregnant. Child support for an ex-mistress of a high-ranking *yakuza*? This wasn't Canada. When I walked into the picture, I provided everything she needed. Who else had regular contact with Goto and his present mistress, combined with a convenient opening in the girlfriend department? Who better to try to get inside a briefcase that might have been stuffed with cash? That probably contained the kind of information a man like Goto would never risk leaving his person? Bank-account numbers, passwords. Combinations to safes. There was no tragic brother, no list of nuclear unfortunates. It was the money Momo wanted. All she needed was a lovestruck *gaijin*.

I began to walk toward them. The little boy noticed me first. Maybe I looked frightening coming out of the sun, or maybe I was the first Westerner he'd ever seen. He grabbed Momo's hand and tugged her around to face me, and her face went dead. Her eyes narrowed and her mouth tightened. Only a few days ago, I'd been nuzzling her behind the ear. She yanked the kid around and walked away. Momo's mother peered at me a moment, gave a little shrug as if to say, *You asked for it* and trudged after them. I felt like I'd walked headfirst into a telephone pole. A concrete, Japanese one.

That night I played the worst gig of my life at the Tom and Mary. Goto didn't show up, which was just as well, because I wasn't sure I could face him. He didn't show up all that week. I began to get the unsettling feeling that he knew a lot more about my comings and goings than was good for me. Each night, I slept with a chair wedged against the door.

By the time Wednesday came around again, I'd made up my mind. I spent an hour before Akiko's lesson in a bar around the corner from her street, working on my resignation speech. No more *yakuza*-girl-friend students. No more *yakuza*, period. My next gig in Goto's bar would be my last. I'd had enough of the fast life. Back to Mrs. Ogawa and her determined Debussy, thank you very much. And another whiskey, please.

But I was on a roll for being wrong. And, of course, I was wrong about my last gig for Goto. I'd never get to play it.

When I got to Akiko's house, the door opened even before I reached it. Akiko was holding a dripping bag of ice to one side of her face.

"You are a fool," she said. The words were mangled, as though she'd just had a root canal. "I thought all men knew."

"Knew what?"

"It's not free."

"What isn't?"

"What you had from Momo. What he got from me. You have to pay."

I wanted to say, *You said* got, *not* gets. But I didn't get the chance. The man with the strange hair appeared in the doorway. Akiko backed into the house, and I stood beside the pond, trying to collect whatever wits I had left after three whiskeys. What had happened here? Had Akiko finally stood up to Goto? Had she also stood up for me? Chisel Face wasn't going to tell me. He touched my elbow and motioned toward the black Mercedes in Akiko's carport. I'd been too drunk and distracted even to see it.

"Please," he said.

Tsukiji

A drive through Tokyo at dusk provides plenty of time for reflection, and the winking on of all that neon does produce a certain magic. Chisel Face and I crawled along. Tokyo traffic was having its nightly heart attack. Wherever we were going, we were going there slowly.

Still, there was plenty to see. A tourist might have enjoyed passing the gardens of the official residence or the car on a turntable in the Maserati dealership. They might have noticed the pet hotels and the electric light pouring out of the concrete canyons of Akihabara and Shinjuku.

But the average tourist wasn't sitting in an air-conditioned Mercedes, counting the rolls of skin on the back of the driver's neck.

Chisel Face was not a patient driver. Every time traffic stopped, he snapped the hand brake on, and the map on the GPS screen was replaced by a sumo wrestling match. Two mountainous men circled the ring, looking for an opening. They looked like enormous babies in diapers. The instant traffic began to move again, Chisel Face snapped the hand brake off, the wrestlers vanished, and we lurched forward. It was starting to make me sick. Only once did I actually see the men connect, and they slammed into each other like stags. The impact straightened both wrestlers into a desperate, locked stagger. Each clutched the other's loincloth for leverage. At least it was a fair fight. I'd already tried my door. I was locked in.

I tried to remember the word for "where." Something that began with *D*. *Dozo*?

That meant "please go ahead," I was pretty sure. Not what my situation called for. Finally it came to me.

"*Doko*?" I said. "Come on, *doko*!"

Chisel Face turned and smiled. He had a single gold tooth. "Tsukiji," he said. The light turned green, the wrestlers vanished in mid-leap and we shot forward again.

Tsukiji was the fish market where Mrs. Ogawa's husband worked. Every tourist had heard of Tsukiji. The rows of deep-frozen tuna like torpedoes. The samurai swords parting thousands of dollars worth of raw, red flesh. The trays and racks and aquariums of fish and shrimp and mollusks, some dead, some still alive. Some, like the eels swimming weakly in their own blood, were somewhere in between. Tsukiji was the most famous fish market in the world. Whatever was going to happen to me, a prime tourist destination seemed the last place to choose. But I didn't know the Japanese word for "why."

The Tsukiji market was b
Bay back when the fish a
from Japanese waters, nc
the world by air. It took another h...
of stop-and-go to get there. My bladder
was bursting from fear and whiskey, and I
wanted to throw up.

Finally the traffic thinned. The roads
became narrower and the shops more
tightly spaced, as though we were going
back in time. Tsukiji was a district, not just
a market, and these streets were its arteries.
Shops sold rubber boots, knives, gloves, ski
masks, meat hooks. They looked like good
places for serial killers to pick up supplies.
There were more restaurants even than
in the food-infested streets of Shibuya. All
of them small, all of them unlikely ever
to see a Western face. But many of them
were shuttered. The streets were oddly
unclogged too. What kind of place was
this, where merchants shut down so early?

We pulled up beside a mountain of white polystyrene boxes piled against a low, weathered concrete building. Nearby, rows of refrigerated trucks idled into the night air. Beyond were freighters and cruise ships and fast ferries riding the surface like water beetles. My door swung open. Chisel Face beckoned me out. I mimed "full bladder," clutching my crotch and swinging from side to side. He pushed me around the mound of boxes, and I peed against the wall of the market while my carsickness subsided. Then he pulled me past a long line of parked forklifts, dug a key out of his pocket and unshackled the hasp on a door I would never even have noticed.

This was not the tourist entrance. Inside, there were no tourists. There were no people of any kind. No fish, no light, just a humid coolness that smelled vaguely of the sea. Tsukiji Market was empty.

If I'd been less focused on jazz, I'd have known that Tsukiji opens at four in the morning. The tuna are auctioned at five. The yellowtail and eels and flounder depart on handcarts, bicycles, trucks, scooters, forklifts. The merchants slurp their noodles in the restaurants until two in the afternoon, and then it's all put to bed until midnight. I'd also have known that a man with Goto's reach was perfectly capable of owning one of the coveted licences to trade in Tsukiji Market. That he could come and go as he wished. And that if he wanted a long, undisturbed chat in the evening, a private office in Tsukiji was the perfect place to do it. We were like lovers visiting a love hotel just to get a little privacy.

Chisel Face pulled out a flashlight and nudged me along a concrete floor. It seemed to run forever beneath low-hanging strings of naked lightbulbs. We passed long tables piled with metal trays and looming band saws. We sidestepped shadowy kiosks where the sellers did their calculations and kept their records. On some of the tables, shallow aquariums gurgled, and in one of them I caught the ghoulish gleam of a startled octopus. The floor was wet. I could see just enough to know that there were countless corridors to either side. If I bolted, I'd be lost in seconds.

Finally we reached a narrow hallway with a row of locked doors. Offices? Tea rooms? Torture chambers? Chisel Face unlocked one of them, kicked the door open and pushed me inside. Then he flicked the light on.

A half dozen chairs ringed a beaten-up wooden table littered with newspapers and magazines. It looked like the kind of place where you waited for your new tires to be installed. Chisel Face selected an inch-thick comic book and settled in to read.

I looked around. Desk, fax machine, grimy telephone, filing cabinet. One door, no window. Outside, a few lonely sea urchins and octopuses. By tomorrow they'd be gone, eaten raw and maybe even wriggling. Whatever was about to happen to me, it couldn't be that bad. A lecture from Goto, some putting me in my place, and I'd be out of here before the next shift showed up. Given the language barrier with Goto and the people who worked for him, most of the ranting would go right over my head. As usual, I'd never know what this was all about.

When the door opened, I realized I was wrong. Yes, it was Goto, and yes, Chisel Face jumped to his feet, ran over to the desk and pulled out the chair. But Goto wasn't alone. Akiko was two steps behind him, her eyes on the floor. She hadn't dumped him after all. Or maybe Goto had dragged her here. A second man followed her. He locked the door, walked to the boardroom table and laid Goto's crocodile briefcase between us. Then he looked at me. It was the third stone face I'd seen today. It was also a face I'd never expected to see again.

Apology

Kaz Nakamura hadn't changed much. He had a more expensive haircut, and he was more formally dressed than when he'd been running his little piano bar in Nanaimo. But the black suit looked good on him. The blank face he was wearing was the same one I'd seen when he walked away from me on a snowy night in downtown Vancouver.

Kaz opened Goto's briefcase and began to lay out his equipment. He might have been assembling a complicated cocktail behind his bar.

"Goto-san has asked me to serve as an interpreter. And to carry out your punishment. He is anxious that there be no misunderstanding."

Goto and Akiko were in shadow, behind the desk. I could smell Goto's aftershave. Chisel Face had taken a chair to a dark corner on the other side of the room. It was just me and Kaz. Misunderstanding? My whole time in Japan had been one big misunderstanding.

"It's not such a coincidence," Kaz said. "There's a limited number of piano bars in Tokyo with *gaijin* performers." He arranged two folded white cloths on one side of the opened briefcase. They were the size of tea towels. "I picked you out immediately. When Goto-san became concerned about your activities, he asked me to help. I also work for Goto-san, a small place in Roppongi. We are in Goto-san's world, not Tokyo."

"My activities?" I'd found my voice, but it didn't sound like me.

"Frank. You're sleeping with a man's mistress. The mother of his son."

"Ex-mistress."

"Not for you to judge, Frank. Whatever she may have told you."

"She told me Goto had killed her brother. Sent him to work in the reactors at Fukushima."

Kaz looked up. "Interesting. Excuse me." He turned to Goto, bowed and spoke rapidly in Japanese. Goto might have smiled, but it was too dark to see. I did hear him laugh. He said a few words to Kaz and adjusted his shades. Kaz turned his attention back to the briefcase.

"He's disappointed in you, Frank. Momo works in a pink salon. Of course owned by Goto-san. As is the Fifteen Love hotel. In case you wondered why Goto-san finally lost patience with you. The rooms do have cameras, Frank."

He took a Japan Airlines ticket out of the case and laid it beside the two white cloths. "You do know what a pink salon is?"

I'd heard of pink salons, but the Japanese sex industry confused me. I was still digesting the idea of being caught on camera. And that the hundred thousand yen had been a slap in the face. I shook my head.

"Pink salon is kind of a sex café. You buy some drinks, a girl comes to your table, you tell her what you want, and she solves your problem. Right there, but discreetly. Momo is very popular, he tells me." He took one more object out of the briefcase, snapped the briefcase shut and set it on the floor.

"One more thing Goto-san wants to know. Before we get started." The object, whatever it was, was inside a black silk bag closed with a drawstring. He laid it on the table between us. It made a soft thunk. "What is it about the briefcase? Goto-san says you've been staring at it for weeks."

"She told me it was full of cash. And a ledger with names of the people he sent to Fukushima." The story sounded ridiculous even to me. All I could think about was Momo servicing lonely Japanese businessmen under the table. Now Kaz was laughing. He relayed my answer to Goto, who snorted.

"Not cash, sorry," Kaz said. "He just likes the way it looks. Maybe he keeps his lunch in there. Comic books. Who knows?" He made a tiny adjustment to the position of the black silk bag. "People start showing up for work in a couple of hours. Let's get it done."

"Get what done?" Now my voice was no more than a croak.

Kaz undid the drawstring and drew out something that looked like a cross between a cook's cleaver and a hatchet. "We call it *nata*. Very sharp, very strong. You can cut wood with it." The thing had a thick rectangular blade, maybe ten inches long, with a deeply beveled edge, like an enormous razor.

The wooden handle curved slightly down. I could imagine chopping kindling with it. But there was no kindling here.

"*Nata* is nothing fancy—you can buy one anywhere. Although you're lucky. This is a very good one. Hold out your arm. Don't worry, I'm not going to chop it off." He grabbed one hand and deftly angled the blade along my forearm. Instantly the metal was sprinkled with hair. I hadn't felt a tickle.

"Japanese steel," Kaz said. "Of course, the best. Now here's what we're going to do." He put the *nata* down, and I snatched my arm back. "You need to apologize to Goto-san."

"That's all? Jesus, why didn't you tell me? What should I say?" I pushed my chair back, and Kaz picked up the *nata* again.

"Not in words, Frank. Words can be insincere. Not true, even. As you've learned." He swung the *nata* gently into the table.

The sharp corner caught in the wood, and the tool stayed there, defying gravity.

"You have to make a gesture. Something that shows you are truly sorry."

"A gesture."

"Put your hand on the table, Frank. The left one."

I bolted out of my chair, and Chisel Face was suddenly behind me. His thumbs went into the muscles at the base of my neck. Maybe he'd been there all the time. Probably I screamed. I wasn't going to get out of this.

"Strong men don't need to be held, Frank. Goto-san would be impressed if you did this yourself. Or his friend will simply break your arm first. Your choice. You've seen how sharp the *nata* is. You won't even feel it, at first. And we will only take one joint." He said a few words in Japanese, and Chisel Face receded. "But you won't be able to play the piano anymore, and the girls won't like you as much. Maybe that's a good thing."

My whole back seemed to be on fire.

"Left hand, little finger. Now, please."

I heard a snuffling sound. Akiko was crying. Goto let her. I slid my left hand forward. It was hard to get the finger to lie flat.

"Try raising your elbow," Kaz said.

Now the finger rested solidly—at least, the first two joints did. I began to shake.

"Try to hold still," said Kaz. "You don't want me to miss." He tugged the *nata* out of the table and carefully reset the point to one side of my finger so that the blade angled above it like a guillotine. He stood, squared his shoulders, put the heel of one hand on the blade and grasped the handle in the other. "Feel free to scream," he said. He rose onto his toes.

I heard a scuffle and in my peripheral vision saw Akiko collared as she tried to bolt. Then Kaz put his weight into the chopper.

Business Class

Kaz was right. I didn't feel much. But I did produce a howl that contained every scale I'd ever practiced, every swinging, sorrowful tune I'd ever played. I couldn't look at my hand. Kaz showed about as much emotion as a person who's just boned a chicken. He shook out one of the white cloths and dropped it over the mess on the table. Then he wiped the *nata* down with the other and put everything back in Goto's briefcase. He tucked the plane ticket into my shirt pocket.

"Keep pressure on it," he said. "You've got ten minutes before it really starts to hurt. And don't forget the fingertip. Sometimes they can sew them back on."

I saw Kaz's back going through the door. I never saw the others leave. I wound the blood-soaked cloth around my hand and stumbled after them. But they had flashlights, and I didn't.

I don't know how long it took me to find my way out of the market. A bank of windows high up near the roof let in enough of the sickly glow of nighttime Tokyo for me to navigate the labyrinth. I was like the ball in a pachinko machine, bouncing off tables and tanks until sheer chance brought me to the right door. I staggered into the humid fug of Tsukiji and collapsed onto a polystyrene container the size of a coffin. Then I clutched my ruined hand to my stomach, doubled over and had a good cry.

I was in a country where I didn't speak the language. Inside a bloody rag was a finger joint to be sewn back on, fast. In the middle of the night. In a hospital that, for all I knew, might look like any other office building. I could be forgiven a few tears of rage and pain and sadness, and there was nobody around to be offended. Or to help. No Kaz doubling back to save me. No Akiko, an angel of mercy in a silver Acura. No Momo cradling my head and assuring me it was all a big misunderstanding. I remembered the pathetic vomiting kid on the train, ignored by everyone, falling to his knees on the platform. That was me now, another disgusting, damaged *gaijin* cast adrift in an indifferent city. I'd become invisible.

And my hand had started to throb. Kaz had been right—the reaction was delayed, but the pain was finally arriving. If I was going to save my finger, I had to know how bad it was. How much blood was I losing? Did I even have the fingertip?

I pulled another squeaking box in front of me, laid my damaged hand on it and carefully loosened the cloth. No fingertip rolled out. Maybe I'd left it on the table, or maybe it had fallen on my way out of the market. Now it was official. I would never play the piano again.

But no fingertip meant no urgency. With applied pressure, the bleeding would stop. Everything that was going to happen to me had happened. I had some wandering around to do until I found a hospital, but the worst was over. Probably the bleeding was slowing down already. It didn't hurt that much.

I lifted my hand and carefully detached the cloth. I steeled myself to look.

My fingertip was in there after all. But it was still attached to the rest of my finger. The blood was coming from a slice across the top of the knuckle, not from a stump. All I needed was a Band-Aid.

I'd been had—again.

I found a taxi outside the warren of shops in Tsukiji and convinced the frightened driver to take me to my apartment. I grabbed my passport, a change of clothes and my stash of tips from Goto's bar. Then I paid the driver the equivalent of a hundred dollars for the ninety-minute ride to Narita International Airport. The sun was rising when I got there, a pale egg yolk in a dirty-yellow sky. I bought some Band-Aids and cleaned myself up in a sparkling washroom. Then I wandered through the shopping concourse until I found a restaurant that served a Western breakfast.

They'd booked me to Vancouver, then through to Nanaimo, and given me just enough time to collect myself and go. But no more. I had to hand it to Kaz—in Japan, even the *yakuza* were efficient. And generous too. When I checked in, I found

I was traveling business class. No baggage? Not a problem, sir. Everyone smiled. Everyone was polite. Uniformed Tokyo Girls bowed me down the jetway.

I was sipping a Sapporo before the rest of the passengers were even seated. I held my aching finger against the cold can. I was going to have a nasty bruise, but that was all. If there'd been a piano on board, I could probably have played it. A text lit up my cell phone just as the plane started to push back. Kaz's timing, as usual, was impeccable.

I owed you one, the message said. That particular *nata* is a collector's item. It was made for a movie about *yakuza* back when there were no digital effects. You can't even see the join where the blade slides up. Sorry if it cut you. Enjoy your flight.

The flight attendant gently relieved me of my beer can and handed me a fresh one. Her smile seemed to come from the heart.

The man in the seat across from me wore headphones the size of grapefruits. Outside on the hot tarmac, three maintenance men bowed as we passed.

"Did you enjoy your stay in Japan?" the attendant asked. The engines started, and the big plane began to lumber forward.

"Parts of it," I said.

Had Kaz pulled me out of the fire? Or had I just been taught a carefully choreographed and exquisitely embarrassing lesson? I typed, Did Goto know? Then I sat back, and the plane began to rumble and rattle toward the runway.

But Kaz never wrote back.

Acknowledgments

My thanks to the Nakagawa family for helping me understand Japan, and also to Ivan Boyadjov and Cody Poulton. As always, David Greer read several versions of the story and asked pointed questions; Ruth Linka, my inestimable editor at Orca Book Publishers, was the crucial and final set of eyes.

BRIAN HARVEY is a marine biologist and writer. Brian's first nonfiction book for a general audience, *The End of the River*, was published in 2008. He is currently finishing a second nonfiction book about sailing around Vancouver Island and is working on several fiction projects. *Tokyo Girl* is the follow-up to *Beethoven's Tenth*, featuring reluctant sleuth Frank Ryan. Brian lives in Nanaimo, British Columbia.

Piano tuner Frank Ryan is paid in kind by an aging music teacher with an old manuscript that turns out to be Beethoven's Tenth Symphony. Launched into a world of intrigue and violence, Ryan, an unlikely sleuth, realizes he must use his wits to conquer his enemies and solve the mystery of the manuscript. In the process Ryan discovers whom he can trust and what he is made of. The first in a series featuring Frank Ryan, Beethoven's Tenth is a smart page-turner.

"The perfect gift for mystery fans."
—*Kirkus Reviews*

RAPID READS
WWW.RAPID-READS.COM